WORD GIRL®

DEVELOPING READER
LEVEL 2
250-750 WORDS

THE BIG BAD BUTCHER

W9-BYO-430

Adapted by Michael Anthony Steele

SCHOLASTIC INC.

New York   Toronto   London   Auckland   Sydney
Mexico City   New Delhi   Hong Kong   Buenos Aires

ISBN-10: 0-545-10039-9
ISBN-13: 978-0-545-10039-7

12 11 10 9 8 7 6 5 4 3 2 1

8 9 10/0

Designed by Angela Jun
Printed in the U.S.A.
First printing, October 2008

Hi! I'm WordGirl.

Captain Huggy Face and I are from the planet Lexicon.

We crash-landed on Earth when I was a baby.

Everyone here knows us as Becky Botsford and Bob.

But secretly, I use my superstrength and word power to fight evil villains.

Word up!

Becky was walking with her friend Scoops.
He was a reporter who wrote for *The Daily Rag.*
"Did you read my article?" he asked.
"Second Main Bank announces free toaster day!"

Over at the bank, a strange man gave a flyer to the security guard.

"Free bobelcue outside," whispered the man.

"What's *bobelcue*?" asked the guard.

"Bobelcue," the man repeated. "Like bobelcue sauce?"

"Oh, *barbecue*!" said the guard. "Hey, everybody! Free barbecue outside!" he shouted.

Everyone ran outside to eat.
Then the strange man snuck into the bank.
The bank's alarm rang.
RRRRRRRRING!

Becky heard the alarm.
In a flash, she turned into WordGirl.
She and Huggy flew to the bank.
"Some guy said there was free barbecue outside," said the guard. "Then he robbed the bank."

"So the barbecue was a diversion," said WordGirl.

The guard looked confused.

"A *diversion* takes your attention away from something important," WordGirl explained.

Scoops arrived.

"Who do you think did this, WordGirl?"

"A barbecue robbery?" she asked. "I have some ideas. . . ."

The next day, the owner of a jewelry shop
was reading *The Daily Rag*.

"Rich Old Lady to Buy Hoboken Diamond,"
he read.

Then a rich old lady entered his store.

"I'd like to buy the Hoboken Diamond,"
she said.

A stranger entered the shop after her.
"Free barbecue!" he shouted.
"Free?!!" shouted the rich old lady.
She dropped the diamond and ran outside.

Becky and Scoops were outside.
They saw a table of barbecue.
"This is just what happened yesterday,"
said Becky.
Then an alarm rang.
RRRRRRRRING!

Scoops looked around for Becky.
But he couldn't find her.
He heard someone shout, "Word up!"
It was WordGirl!

"Hold it right there!" ordered WordGirl.
"This time your diversion failed."

"I didn't serve any diversion," the Butcher
said. "Only ribs and chicken."

The Butcher held out his hands.
"Pot Roast Attack!"
WordGirl was trapped inside a pile of meat.
The Butcher escaped through the front window.
CRASH!

"Hmmm . . . I wrote about the bank and the jewelry shop. Then they were robbed," Scoops said.

"I've got it! The Butcher uses your stories to plot his crimes!" WordGirl said. "I have an idea. . . . "

The Butcher sat in his secret den.
"I wonder what I should steal next."
He read Scoops's latest article in *The Daily Rag*.
"Vic's Vegetarian Restaurant Makes Millions."

The Butcher ran into the restaurant.
"Free barbecue!"
"But I already have food," said a customer.
The Butcher only saw white cubes.
"It's tofu. We don't eat meat,"
said the customer.

WordGirl and Huggy flew into the restaurant.
"It's over, Butcher!"
"Did you know these people don't eat
meat?" the Butcher asked.
"That's what *vegetarian* means," she said.

"You're not getting away this time!" said WordGirl.

"Oh yeah?" asked the Butcher. "Sausage Cyclone!"

"Huggy, help!" shouted WordGirl.

Huggy grabbed a square of tofu.
He flung it at the Butcher.
SPLAT!
It hit him right in the face.

The Butcher was dazed.
"Sausage Cyclone!" he shouted again.
But nothing happened.

"Tofu blocks his power!" shouted WordGirl.
So Huggy threw more.
SPLAT! SPLAT! SPLAT!
The Butcher fell to the ground.

Scoops rushed in.
"I've got my next headline: Barbecue Bandit Stopped!" he shouted.

It was another victory for WordGirl and Captain Huggy Face!

Thanks to the power of the press — and the power of tofu!

25

Hello, I'm Beau Handsome! Are you ready to solve some puzzles? Of course you are!

In our story, meat gave WordGirl a lot of trouble. Cross out all the M's, E's, A's, and T's below. Then use the rest of the letters to spell out a message from WordGirl herself!

M A T T W E E M A T E O T A M E R E
D T E A A M E A T A U E E E T M A P
_ _ _ _   _ _ !

Captain Huggy Face certainly scrambled the Butcher's plans with that tofu attack. See if you can unscramble these words!

Words

LYF   _ _ _

PEAC   _ _ _ _

MALRA   _ _ _ _ _

HYGUG   _ _ _ _ _

Clues

How WordGirl travels

It drapes over WordGirl's back

This loud thing went off during the robberies

WordGirl's lovable sidekick

Here's another one! Using more words from the story, fill in the squares down and across.

Across
2. Something that you barbecue
3. The name WordGirl's parents call her
5. Nickname of the reporter who's friends with WordGirl
6. Captain Huggy Face's secret identity
8. This takes someone's attention away from something important
9. *The Daily* ___
10. Another way to say "bad guy." (Hint: The Butcher is one of these)

Down
1. Lots of money is kept here
3. Name of the villain who attacks WordGirl with meat
4. Superhero who fights with words, also known as Becky Botsford
5. Spicy links of meat. The Butcher sometimes uses this to attack

WordGirl searches for super villains and criminals everywhere. Do you have what it takes to search for these hidden words?

You can find words by looking up, forward, backwards, and diagonally.

```
M Z Z R X C X J U X
K H Y W P J D F S W
D N N X W T O X F L
G Z A Z N T O K C T
Z Y K B Y D S N A M
C W N I A L L I V E
U F T S A O R N X A
Z B U T C H E R U T
F E O A N B I X J K
B A R B E C U E X G
```

Words to find:

BANK   BARBECUE   BUTCHER
MEAT   ROAST   TOFU
VILLAIN

Now try your hand at some "worduko" puzzles! Fill in the grids below so that every row, column, and box contains the letters named under the board. The diagonal will spell out a word!

t			o
u		t	f
	u		t
f		o	u

letters: fuot

	k		
	a		b
k		n	

letters: nabk

Answer Key

Congratulations!

Page 26:
Cross-out Code:
Word Up!

Word Scramble:
FLY
CAPE
ALARM
HUGGY

Page 27:

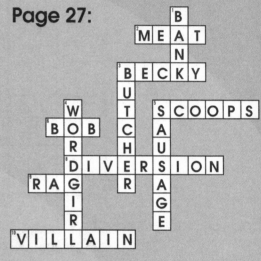

Crossword answers:
- 1 (down) BANNER
- 2 (across) MEAT
- 3 (across) BECKY
- 3 (down) BUTCHER
- 4 (down) WORDGIRL
- 5 (down) SAUSAGE
- 5 (across) SCOOPS
- 6 (across) BOB
- 7 (across) DIVERSION
- 8 (across) RAG
- 10 (across) VILLAIN

Page 28:

Word search grid:

M	Z	Z	R	X	C	X	J	U	X
K	H	Y	W	P	J	D	F	S	W
D	N	N	X	W	T	O	X	F	L
G	Z	A	Z	N	T	O	K	C	T
Z	Y	K	B	Y	D	S	N	A	M
C	W	N	I	A	L	L	I	V	E
U	F	T	S	A	O	R	N	X	A
Z	B	U	T	C	H	E	R	U	T
F	E	O	A	N	B	I	X	J	K
B	A	R	B	E	C	U	E	X	G

Page 29:

t	f	u	o
u	o	t	f
o	u	f	t
f	t	o	u

b	k	a	n
n	a	k	b
k	b	n	a
a	n	b	k